SOUP IN LOVE

YEARLING BOOKS/YOUNG YEARLINGS/YEARLING CLASSICS are designed especially to entertain and enlighten young people. Patricia Reilly Giff, consultant to this series, received her bachelor's degree from Marymount College and a master's degree in history from St. John's University. She holds a Professional Diploma in Reading and a Doctorate of Humane Letters from Hofstra University. She was a teacher and reading consultant for many years, and is the author of numerous books for young readers.

For a complete listing of all Yearling titles,
write to Dell Readers Service,
P.O. Box 1045, South Holland, IL 60473.

SOUP IN LOVE

ROBERT NEWTON PECK

Illustrated by Charles Robinson

A Yearling Book

Soup in Love is dedicated to my many Italian friends, in Italy, and in America, who may find and enjoy my hidden Italiano humor. *Santé* . . . to red, white, and green . . .

And to *amore*.

ROBERT NEWTON PECK

One

"Here it is," said Soup, "and here we go."

It was a Saturday afternoon.

Earlier, we both had ached to go to the movies, the usual Saturday double-cow feature, but neither of us could scrape up a dime.

Now we were standing in one of Learning's two back alleys and thinking about heading for home. And chores. The weather had surprisingly warmed, seeing as it was the first day of February. Here in Vermont, a winter afternoon can darken early. The sky beamed no sunshine. It was grayer than a granny.

Pale as pewter.

Soup Vinson's farm was next to ours, just uproad, so we'd soon be trudging homeward together. At school we always sat side by side, until Miss Kelly had to separate us, which was her daily joy. Or so we thought.

"Rob," said Soup, "maybe we'll enjoy ourselfs a shorter route to home if we duck through our secret shortcut."

"S'pose," I reluctantly agreed.

Approaching a very narrow passage between two aging three-story buildings, Filbert's Warehouse and a deserted Peterson's Paint Factory, we paused at the mouth of a long gap. Less than two feet wide.

A canyon between two windowless walls.

High above us, uneven rims showed overhanging snow, dripping with today's thaw. This confining shortcut was a place I didn't like to cut through. It was spooky. Few kids used it. Mama repeatedly warned me to beware of rickety old buildings, especially a rotten old relic like Peterson's Paint Factory. Soup's mother had given him a similar lecture.

Pointing up, I said, "Lots of melting snow up yonder, Soup." As he looked skyward, I added, "It might be silly to chance cutting through here. If that snow falls, it'll bury us alive."

Above was a long slender strip of colorless sky. Icicles dripped from both gutters. The canyon appeared wider up there than down here, because both buildings had listed and sagged.

Soup stopped.

Turning to me, he said, "Robert, a pinch of danger is what sprinkles ginger on the apple pie of life."

"Okay," I sighed. "But let's hustle."

"You go first," said Soup, stepping politely aside. This was unusual. Soup Vinson, a year and four months my senior, always went first.

"Why *me*?"

"Because you're thinner and quicker. If I go first, you'll only overtake me, we'll trip, and the impact could dislodge all that loose snow up yonder."

"Either we both go," I said firmly, "or I'm going to chicken out to the long way around. The *safe* route."

"We're both going," Soup vowed. "Word of honor."

"Good."

"Go."

As I apprehensively started through the slushy alley, a sixty- or seventy-foot gallop, a twitching glance over my shoulder assured me that Soup was following. Sure as my name was Robert Newton Peck, I rarely trusted Luther Wesley Vinson.

Forward I splashed through the slush.

Behind me, I heard the close spattering of Soup Vinson's boots. We were, I was estimating, about halfway through the narrow canyon when something happened. It was a strange noise. Bad news. It seemed to echo between the tight walls of our shortcut.

Then it hit.

A big round snowmass fell from above, off the warehouse roof. Its size would have served as the bottom snowball for a very large snowman. Or a small planet.

SSSPPPPLLLLLLAAAAAATTTTT.

Landing, it exploded directly in front of me, hitting with

force. I braked in a breath. Then another big ball fell. Another. And still another.

SPLAT. SPLAT. SPLAT.

In seconds, our passage had been totally blocked by a high mound of wet, slippery snow. Another one fell.

SPLAT.

"Rob, I'm turning back."

"Me too. Let's get out of here."

But then, as we reversed our direction, it all happened for a second time. More balls fell crashing to the alley floor, blocking us. This wasn't natural. Something, or someone, was causing it all.

SPLAT. SPLAT. SPLAT. SPLAT. SPLAT.

Looking up, I saw nothing.

"We're trapped, Soup."

"Cornered."

"We can't advance or retreat."

"Rob, this is serious."

"I know. If we die we'll miss *chores.*"

Farm kids know. There's no excuse for reporting to the barn tardy at chore time. "Cows do not wait," Papa told me, "for saints or sinners." Nor do mothers or fathers.

"It's a caution," said Soup. "We could be bottled up here for the entire month of February."

No, I thought in panic. *No.* NO.

Of all months, February was most important. Today was February the first. Thirteen more days. Then I'd present my reverent offering (homemade in red and white paper and probable glue-stained) to that very special someone who made my heart flutter. Pulse to race. Glands to pant an emotional polka.

Norma Jean Bissell.

"Norma Jean," I softly breathed, barely trusting my unworthy lips to utter her name, in humble devotion.

Eyeing me with a glance that threatened a stomach upset, Soup said, "How can you think of *trivia* at a time like this?" Hands on his hips, he asked me, "Could our predicament be worse?"

It got worse.

We heard a hollow laugh.

"No," Soup moaned, "it can't be."

Glancing up quickly, I caught a glimpse of a face, a sneer with fangs. Yellow eyes. My throat gulped in terror. Lurking above us perched the most feared half-grown predator in the Western Hemisphere. A kid with industrial-strength fists.

Together, Soup and I swallowed, trembled, and spoke the eleven evil letters that could curdle the blood of every kid in Learning:

Janice Riker

There she was, her canine overbite leering at her two trapped victims, her nostrils flaring to the size of twin hockey pucks. "Gotcha," said Janice, flashing her most endearing smile with all the warmth of Siberia.

She was right.

She had us.

Her face disappeared. Soup and I waited, of course, as we had no escape. No exit. None.

Alas, no hope.

A large economy-size missile began to appear on the brink of the warehouse roof, directly above the cherubic innocence of our upturned faces. There it was, one enormous snowball, far larger than any of those that had fallen to imprison us.

It was Janice Riker's finale.

The capper.

"No," whispered Soup.

"Yes," I differed. "She's going to bombard us with that big white blockbuster."

Soup, always the optimist, said, "Perhaps the two of us can catch it."

I looked at my pal.

"*Catch* it? It'll weigh a ton. How did Janice ever make so big a snowball?"

"Easy," said Soup in a hapless tone. "She rolled it around in circles, pushing it, on the warehouse roof. It's flat up there on top. That's how. You know how strong Janice is."

I knew.

Rigid in horror, we waited.

We couldn't see it all. Nowhere near. Only a slice of it. As they say in all those seafaring stories at the Arctic Circle . . . *just the tip of the iceberg.* Almost all of Janice's giant snowball was out of sight, yet ready, waiting for a push into gravity. A bomb, with Janice at the trigger.

Norma Jean Bissell would never rapturously receive my valentine (yet unmade). Its giver would be nailed beneath Fate's hammer like a helpless tack.

I couldn't see Janice.

"Where," asked Soup, "did she go?"

She returned. In each hand she brandished a ten-quart pail. Both appeared full.

"I got water," yelled Janice.

"Rob," said Soup. "you and I are about to receive one chiller of an ice-cold shower."

We braced ourselves. Yet no shower came. Instead, she dumped all the water, both buckets, on her giant snowball, now an asteroid of cold slush. Janice disappeared again. But her snowball did not. It grew. Looking up, my neck aching, I now saw a quarter of it, then a half, and finally *all*.

For a split second, the gigantic white sphere seemed suspended in space. Then it fell.

"Duck," said Soup.

There was nowhere to duck. A month ago, during our last scoot through this forbidden canyon, I recalled seeing some sort of a door. Above me, an Alp continued to fall . . . bigger . . . wetter . . . faster. Closer it fell. Close. Then closer. Closing my eyes, I mumbled my jiffy prayer, as there was no time for a lengthy devotion.

SSPPPLLLLOOOOOSSSSSHHH.

The ball of slush stopped.

Without hitting us, there it seemed to stay, only six feet above our heads, dripping, yet solidly wedged between the two slanting walls. We were wet, yet unharmed. But the snowball was thawing, drip after drip after determined drip.

"We will drown," I whispered.

"Not a chance," said Soup. "Instead, night will fall, it'll turn a lot colder as it always does, and, here in the dark, we'll merely freeze to death."

Aunt Carrie would do milking.

Two

"Hello out there."

I heard a familiar voice.

Turning, I saw who it was. So did Soup. Both of us smiled as we saw an open door and a friendly face with a long, droopy white moustache. A face we'd seen often at Joe's Diner.

It was Joe.

Even though he had been born in Naples, Mr. Joe Spazzatura had resided here in our happy town of Learning for most of his life. His hair was as white as his apron, and his smile was always ready to greet a friend, or a stranger.

"What you boys do out here?" he asked, a look of concern on his face. He didn't ask in a hostile way.

"Mr. Spazzatura," said Soup quickly, "we, who were about to die, salute you."

Soup saluted.

So did I.

"Never mind that," said Joe. "You can't stay in danger out here in this alley. Come in. Quick."

Needless to say, into the haven of Filbert's Warehouse we scooted. Safe at last. And no Janice Riker. We both thanked Joe again and again.

"Hey, I got something new to show you," said Joe. The old gentleman held up two fingers. "I got *two* things. Come look."

We followed Mr. Spazzatura.

First, he showed us something really tiny, and quite cute, a little stray kitten that he had found and adopted. Its home would be his home, at Joe's Diner. There, he told us, his kitten would become a happy cat.

I smiled, inside and out.

Joe, I knew, was the nicest and kindest person in Learning. If people were hungry, yet without money, they could always get a good hot meal at Joe's. On the house. No charge. Even though Mr. Joe Spazzatura never attended church, as far as I was concerned, he'd rescued his share of people as well as pets. Perhaps this was why his clothes were so shabby and his smile so bright.

Eat at Joe's was the official advertising slogan for Joe's Diner & Diesel Fuel Stop. Truckers welcome. As you sat at Joe's old battered counter, on one of the shabby stools, there was a little sign on his wall:

A MAN TAKES TO HEAVEN ONLY WHAT
HE GIVES AWAY ON EARTH.

But not many paying customers ate at Joe's. A few years ago, when the Learning Lead Mill was operating, the millworkers ate there. No longer. After the mill closed down, few folks bothered to climb Dugan's Hill to Eat at Joe's. The diner looked worse than its proprietor and badly needed a coat of paint.

"How's business?" Soup asked him.

Joe shrugged.

"Not so hot. Right now, it's a Depression. So maybe business isn't so good anywhere in town."

"We hope your business gets better," I said.

Soup agreed. "We certain do."

Joe allowed us to pet his kitten and then asked us to think of a name for her. A February name. We promised we'd work on it.

"Now," said Joe, "maybe you boys wonder why I'm down here at Filbert's Warehouse, and not up a hill at the diner."

"Yes," I said, as the four of us (including Joe's new kitten, which he gently carried) were walking among the huge crates and boxes and cartons inside the warehouse. "How come you're down here?"

Joe's face brightened. "Wait until you see. Mr. Filbert called me up with the news. Very big news."

"What is it?" Soup asked.

"Follow," he said, crooking a finger.

Turning a corner, we all came to a very large packing box, a white crate with Eat at Joe's painted on the side in red letters.

"A big box?" Soup asked.

"No. The big news is *inside.*"

"What's in there?" I asked.

Joe smiled proudly.

"It's a brand-new secondhand refrigerator. She's come on a noon freight train. I haven't unpacked it yet." He sighed. "My old icebox give out. She quit. Died of old age."

"Sure is big," I said.

Soup agreed. "Biggest box I ever saw." Soup walked all the way around it and reappeared. "By the way, Mr. Spazzatura, after you open it up, what are you going to do with this great big crate?"

"Nothing." Joe shrugged. "I got a no use for it."

Soup asked, "Are you taking it to The Dump?"

Joe slowly nodded. And then he asked us a very promising question. "Would you boys like to have it? For keeps? Maybe for a fort or a clubhouse. You want it?"

"*Yes,*" said Soup, "if you please."

Mr. Spazzatura clapped Soup Vinson gently on the shoulder. "Okay, it's a deal. It's all yours. *After* I get somebody to truck it to The Dump."

"Thanks," said Soup, "thanks a lot!"

But then Mr. Spazzatura raised a warning finger. "After you're through with it, back it goes. I don't want no Eat at Joe's crate to be a eyesore."

"You have our solemn word," said Soup.

"Good boy," said Joe.

On the way home, we walked up Dugan's Hill with Mr. Spazzatura, waiting for him every few feet. Halfway up stood his eatery, Joe's Diner, where we stopped. Joe gave his kitten some heated milk, and a raisin cookie to Soup and to me.

At one time, the diner had been a real railroad car. In fact, it now rested its iron wheels on two railroad rails that tracked down the hill and into town. There, the rails ended at a blank wall, at Peterson's Paint Factory.

"So long, boys," said Joe with a wave. "Stop in soon if you get hungry. I always got a pancake for a pal. Or maybe you can say hello to my old white horse, Black Thunder."

We promised to stop by.

Joe stood there, in his spotty apron, petting his new little kitten. "If you got food," Joe said, "you got a mouse. But . . . if you got a cat, you no got a mouse. You got food."

On our way home, Soup was in deep thought.

"Okay," I asked, "what is it?"

"What's what?"

"How are you going to use that extra-big refrigerator crate, once it's empty?"

Soup sighed.

"Rob, old sport, I don't yet actual know."

I smelled *trouble.* Hurriedly, almost in panic, I said, "Well, whatever it is you're planning, I don't guess I want to be in on it. No way. Not even a crumb's worth."

Soup stopped.

Turning, he stared at me.

"Robert Newton Peck, do you mean to stand there in the road and tell me that you're not in the least bit interested in somebody named . . . Norma Jean Bissell?"

I made a face. "What does Norma Jean have to do with some useless empty crate, with no refrigerator in it?"

"Nothing," said Soup.

"Nothing?"

"Well," he said, "not quite yet."

On we walked, toward home.

"However," said Soup, packing a snowball and throwing it high in the air (at least a good fifteen feet), "there's something uncanny about that crate. Maybe it'll come in handy."

We kept walking.

"For what?" I asked Soup.

"Well, I can't decide just yet. Rob, old tiger, opportunity doesn't always waltz with inspiration." Leaping off the road, Soup Vinson balanced himself on the top rail of a fence, arms extended and waving for balance. "But when my big idea final strikes . . . at least we'll have a box to contain it."

I watched him walking the fence rail. Several times he fell, but he wouldn't quit.

Truth be known, there wasn't any other guy in the whole U.S.A. that I'd rather pick for a pal. There was only *one* Luther Wesley Vinson. The world couldn't have survived *two.* Trouble was, I knew his brain was about to cackle and lay an egg.

Soup, over the years, had plunged the two of us into so much hot water that I was starting to feel like a teabag.

Three

"Soap," said Miss Kelly.

Our teacher, the only teacher in our modest one-room schoolhouse, was marching me to the corner washstand.

"Robert Newton Peck," she informed me, handing me a small brown object with which I had rarely been too familiar, "this is soap. Octagon. And it won't hurt a bit."

As I faked a wash, or tried to, Miss Kelly stood nearby in a supervisory capacity.

While I was returning the bar of Octagon to its puddle of

gloppy goo in the soap dish, I was restrained. "Under your fingernails," she said.

Her voice was not unkind. Merely insistent. Several times a year, Miss Kelly confided in all twenty-eight of us (our entire student body) that she fervently believed in three principles. They were prominently featured on a framed needlepoint sampler that hung on the wall behind her desk:

Scholarship, Manners, and Soap

These, she insisted, were a trio of sterling Vermont virtues, all of which would guide our little feet onward, and upward, to that most worthy of goals . . . a shining character.

Beneath my thumbnail, Miss Kelly was now pointing out, lay a black crescent of muck, last summer's souvenir of our farm's richest topsoil. To me, this dark curve was ever-present, so I presumed this entrenched silty furrow was part of my thumb.

Miss Kelly disagreed.

My quarter ring of good earth slowly surrendered to Octagonal omnipotence.

"Am I done?" I asked, preparing to bolt.

"Not so fast," Miss Kelly said.

Without warning, and striking like a cobra, she soaped the washrag and attacked the back of my neck, buffing it harder than if waxing a truck fender. Finally, having attained hygienic standards that would have made the Mayo Brothers gasp in tribute, I was allowed to return to my bench, beside Soup Vinson.

The pair of us (until every morning around ten o'clock, when we had to be separated by Miss Kelly) shared one desk. Leaning close, Soup sniffed at me.

"Rob, you smell different."

"I do? In what way?"

"Sort of . . . new."

"How did I smell before?"

"Used." He grinned. "By a previous owner."

Up front, Miss Kelly had also returned to her desk, and picked up her pointer. No, not a dog. A long stick of wood that she used to point to things that were often boring and useless.

Miss Kelly now became overly interested in a mysterious something or other called The Equator. It was only *a dotted line* around the globe (at the fattest part) that nobody could actual see. Yet some Mr. Columbus guy always knew when he'd crossed it. Perhaps when he followed it, on a fast ship, he could really *tear along the dotted line*.

"So," she was now lecturing, "as we can see on the globe, the ocean separating Africa from Europe is called the . . ."

I wasn't listening.

Instead of paying attention to our teacher, I was peeking over my book, *Frontiers of Geography*, to study other more interesting contours.

Reverently I sighed her name.

"Norma Jean Bissell."

Turning to me, Soup made his favorite digestive noise. A real flutterbooper. "Rob," he said, "you'd better watch your step." He nudged me for emphasis. "She's a *girl*," he hissed.

"And girls are after only one thing. A ring . . . in your nose."

Miss Kelly, I was sudden aware, was staring at Soup and me.

"Luther and Robert," she began with a sigh.

Our teacher must have really liked our names, because never a day passed by when she didn't say them, in conjunction.

Ten seconds later, Luther Vinson and Rob Peck had been ordered up front to the blackboard. There we both stood, chalk in hand, writing the words on adjacent black squares. Soup on his. Me on mine. Miss Kelly was dictating.

I wrote:

> Polight stoodints remane
> silunt and atent if wile a
> teecher atemps to teech with
> out Anacin.

We finished, replaced the chalk in its dust-filled tray, and then, to impress Miss Kelly, wiped our floury hands on our pants.

"Read it," Miss Kelly commanded. But seeing as we both started to read silently, she added, "Aloud, please."

We read it.

"What does it mean?" she asked us.

Soup answered. "Uh, it means Rob ought to pay more attention to you than to Norma Jean."

I could have murdered him.

Norma Jean Bissell's face flushed pinker than The Pool

Parlor's new MEN ONLY neon sign. And on my cheek you could have grilled a frankfurter.

Soup, however, was grinning, happier than a pig in mud. Before I could even think of a cuss word, he quickly added, "It applies to me too, Miss Kelly. I was whispering to Rob and we're both sorry. We'd like to apologize."

It was obvious that Soup had noticed the pointer in Miss Kelly's hand. It could do more than point. The wood was solid hickory and a lean thirty-incher. A weapon that our teacher could whip up faster than my favorite cowboy, Buck Jones, could fan a Colt .44.

"We're sorry, Miss Kelly," I said hurriedly, eyeing the pointer as I spoke.

"Are you?" she asked me.

"Yes'm. And we won't do it again."

"At least not today," said Soup. "Or tomorrow. Or next week. Yet it would be dishonest to promise that we'll be perfect. But on days that you might be suffering from a headache, Rob and I will try to be extra indulgent."

"Yes," I said. "And we'll wash."

"Thank you," she said, "for understanding that your teacher is also a human being, not a perfect one."

"By the way," Soup asked Miss Kelly, "on what days of the week do you usual have a headache?"

She answered Soup's question promptly, and with just a hint of a forgiving smile.

"Monday through Friday."

Four

Miss Kelly's day got better.

Because, about ten minutes later, a car honked, and then Miss Kelly's best friend came exploding through the door. Someone who often brought excitement.

It was Miss Boland, our county nurse.

Bursting from her heavy woolen coat, scarf, and a thick pair of mittens, Miss Boland hung her wraps on a door peg, then turned to face us all. Her nursing uniform was so white, so clean, and so starched that it could bully any bacterium into total submission and retreat.

Our county nurse was all smiles.

"Guess," she said. "I'll just wager that not a one of you could imagine exactly where I've been, and what I saw. Guess!"

"We give up," said Miss Kelly. "Tell us."

"Well, early this morning and away before light, I cranked up the Hoover, and drove up north to Thurgood. You won't believe what I saw." Miss Boland, despite her ponderosity (a size smaller than a great white whale), almost danced.

"No," said Miss Kelly, "we won't believe it."

"Okay, I'll tell you. From one end of their village to the other, along the main street, the entire town of Thurgood is . . . *decorated*."

"For what?" asked our teacher.

"Valentine's Day!"

As Miss Boland nearly shouted those two words, I stole a hurried glance at Norma Jean Bissell. She also looked at me. My heart soared like a fly ball.

"Yessiree," said our nurse, "lots of fresh snow and little hearts hanging near to everywhere. On everything. Even the dogs. Why, the whole village is a red-and-white picture postcard."

"It must really be pretty," Miss Kelly said.

Pacing to and fro in our school, up front, Miss Boland was gesturing wildly with her hands. "*Pretty* isn't the word," she said. "*Spectacular* would be more like it. And"—she turned to Miss Kelly—"I could easily guess how they pulled it off."

"How?"

"A year or so ago, old Mr. Barley Grisholm passed away. He must've been pushing ninety if he was a day . . . and he remembered the town in his will. Or so folks seem to claim.

That's how they could afford to buy or make all their decorations. And for good reason. Mr. Grisholm was born on Valentine's Day."

Miss Kelly took a step toward her friend. "You know, it would be nice if *we* could do something special to brighten up our winter. Here in Learning."

"Right." Miss Boland snapped her fingers. Then her smile melted to a look of concern. "But we don't have any funds in the town treasury . . . leastwise, not a penny to fritter away on little frilly hearts. Too bad our Christmas decorations are all packed up and salted away. At least some of them are red and white. Suitable colors. But no hearts."

"They're all stored away?" Miss Kelly asked.

Miss Boland nodded. "Yes, in Lem Wheeler's cowshed. Except for the two big candy-cane contraptions. They're so old they ought to be pitched at The Dump. But I'd hate to just throw 'em away."

"Where are they?"

"Oh," said Miss Boland, "Lem and I decided to save 'em, so we found a place, exactly a hundred yards away. I know, because I paced it off."

"Are they real candy?" Soup asked.

"Shucks, no," said Miss Boland. "They're all wooden, but look like candy canes, because Porter Phelps and I painted them alternately red and white, like a peppermint cane."

"I remember," said Miss Kelly. "They were standing up, as candy canes, outside the gate on the village square."

"Correct," said Miss Boland.

Soup was quiet. Thinking, no doubt.

"Now then," said Miss Boland, "while driving my Hoover home from Thurgood, I came up with an interesting idea."

"Tell us," Miss Kelly said. "We're all ears."

"First," said Miss Boland, raising one finger to point at the ceiling, "we ask everyone in town to make a red heart, any size at all, and hang it on a lamppost, or a tree, or across a front door."

"That could work," said Miss Kelly. "In fact, it could be done in a day. We'll help construct a few red hearts here at school." She turned to us. "Won't we, class?"

"Yes'm," we responded.

"Good," said Miss Boland. Holding up two fingers, she added, "Number two, we'll award a prize to the person or persons that create the most unusual valentine."

"A prize?" Soup quickly asked.

"Right you are. Perhaps," said Miss Boland, "we can give valentines to all our friends, and the spirit of love will spread through our entire community. We could have a box, with a slot in the top, positioned in the village park, to deposit our valentines. Then, on February fourteenth, we open the box and pass 'em out. I'll find all the local names in the telephone book, so everyone'll get a valentine, one way or another."

Soup turned to me.

"Rob, we ought to make sure that we send valentines to Miss Boland, and to Miss Kelly." He smirked. "Can you think of anyone else?"

With longing, I gazed at Norma Jean Bissell.

"Soup, I'm still sore at you, you rat, for what you said in front of everybody."

"I'm sorry, Rob. All in fun."

"How come *you're* never fascinated by girls?"

"I'm too bright. Besides," said Soup, "for the next ten days, you and I ought to unite our talents for a purpose."

"And what's that?"

"Robert, old top, you and I will win the prize!"

"For the most unusual valentine?"

Soup nodded. "An idea is forming in my brain."

Trouble!

I could now inhale disaster easier than I could smell Octagon soap. His plan, I was already presuming, wouldn't stand a chance of our winning the prize. All it would do is dump us into deviltry's dungeon. Furthermore, it might prevent my spending a few cherishable moments on Valentine's evening in the company of Norma Jean.

"Soup, I don't like it."

"You don't like Valentine's Day?"

"No. I mean yes. What I'm objecting to is how you're going to dream up some tomfool scheme that'll ruin it. My hair still has sparks from your last crazy invention. Remember? You almost got us electrocuted."

Soup nodded. "Oh, I remember. At least we learned that a couple of big battery-driven electric fans, upside down in the water, won't propel a canoe."

"Okay, I want your promise. You won't ruin Miss Boland's coming-up Valentine's Day festivities. Give me your solemn word."

Soup raised his right hand.

"I promise. No canoe."

Five

Soup and I stayed after school.

Not that we had to. It was Soup's idea.

"Rob, let's help Miss Kelly tidy up," he had suggested, "because we gave her so much grief today."

So we remained to empty the wastebasket, whack the dust off both of the erasers (by whacking them on each other), and wash the blackboard with a damp rag. Once it was wet, the blackboard looked a lot blacker, and it was sort of fun to watch it melt slowly dry. Like a cloudy day becoming sunny.

"We're final finished, Miss Kelly," I said.

Sitting at her desk, tucking a few books and pencils into

the side drawers, our teacher pretended to frown at us. Just in fun. We knew she liked us. And we liked her a lot.

"Luther and Robert," she said at last, "you both have so much inside you. Yet I admit not knowing what it is. And I fear to ask."

"Thanks," said Soup.

Standing, she shook hands with us, offering us a genuine smile. "Years and years ago," she said, "a senior teacher advised me to hug children the most on days when they least deserve it." Bending down, she hugged us.

"I guess there'll be days," I admitted, "when you might have to hug Soup and me a whole lot."

Miss Kelly sighed. "Quite," she said.

As I talked to Miss Kelly, allowing that I was sorry we'd acted up worrisome, Soup was pawing at something on our teacher's desk. I saw him pick it up. And grin.

"Miss Kelly," he said, "would you consider doing Rob and me a very small favor . . . please?"

Slowly she arched her right eyebrow with a well-practiced gesture, one of silent suspicion. "Perhaps," she said with caution. "Yet it depends on how you intend to employ my ball of string."

"Rob and I," said Soup, tossing the ball into the air so I could catch it, "need some string. Quite a bit of it."

"We do?" I asked Soup.

He nodded, flashing me a sly wink.

"How much," Miss Kelly asked, "do you need? If it's half a mile for a kite, the answer is *no*. Your last kite blew into Lake Champlain, carrying most of my string with it."

"To be straight-out truthful," Soup said, "we sort of probable need to use it all."

"All of it?"

"Yes'm. But," he quickly added, "we're not intending to
keep any of the string." He smiled. "Not even an inch."

"When," asked Miss Kelly, "do you plan to return it?"

"Tomorrow morning."

"Promise?"

With a hand covering his heart (and his shirt) Soup promised.

"What do we need the string for, Soup?"

"To measure. And to make a circle."

Miss Kelly walked the pair of us to the door. "I should have
guessed," she said.

Once out the door, Soup said that we'd best go downroad
to the high school football field.

"Why?" I asked.

"You'll see."

I saw.

At the football field, which was covered with snow, Soup
handed me the one loose end of string. "Hold it," he said,
"and don't let go." Carrying the ball of string, Soup Vinson
started backing up. He backed all the way through the snow
to the other end of the football field. The ball of string, as I
could easily see, became smaller and smaller. Until there
was no ball.

Only a wad.

And then another loose end.

"Hey," yelled Soup, "what a lucky break. The string is just

about the same length as a football field, from goal line to goal line, one hundred yards. So I won't have to cut it."

"Good," I said, wondering what prank Soup was playing.

Slowly he came toward me, rolling the string into a sloppy ball. Because he was walking faster than he could roll, by the time he reached me, there wasn't really a ball of string. Merely a large unruly snarl.

"That's a mess," I said.

"It doesn't matter, Rob. Because once we get to Mr. Lem Wheeler's place, we only have to unwind it again."

"What for?"

"To swing a big circle."

"Oh."

It didn't take long to get to Mr. Wheeler's, as he lived near the high school. Yet I still was curious as to what my pal, Luther Wesley Vinson, was planning.

Soup pointed.

"There it is."

"There what is?" I asked.

"What we're looking for. Mr. Lem Wheeler's cowshed. It'll serve as our center point."

As he raced to it, I followed. Jumping up on a big barrel, Soup peeked through a gap between two gray board slats. "Ah," he said, "this is it." He jumped down.

"What's in there?"

"Christmas decorations."

"Hold it," I said firmly. "We're *not* going to steal or borrow or use any of that Christmas stuff. If we did, Miss Boland would have a Holstein."

Soup smiled.

"Right," he said, "we won't do it."

"We won't?" It was too bounteous to believe.

"No," he said, "we don't need any of this stuff. But we're wasting precious time, Rob, so up on the barrel you go. From there, you can step on that drainspout, and then climb up on the cowshed roof. Up, old tiger, up."

I took a deep breath.

"Why?"

Soup sighed. "Because the center has to hold one end of the string. Rob, you're the center."

It was useless to argue. Soup Vinson obviously had an idea in mind, about making some silly old circle. With *string*. So up I went, holding the string end in my teeth as I climbed. Madness, I was concluding. Utter madness.

Looking down at my crazy pal, I asked, "Now what?"

"It's a surprise. So don't let go."

Turning, he ran with the string until he was a hundred yards away and Miss Kelly's long length of string was a straight line. He looked in a barn. Then moving to his left, he searched a garage, a vacant house, another garage, part of The Dump, and a gully under a road. Crossing a field, he looked in more places. But I noticed something odd. Soup, more or less, was keeping the string pulled almost tight. And always moving to his left, managing to stay the same distance from me atop Mr. Wheeler's cowshed.

Soup was compassing a circle that nobody would ever see. Why? I'd never know. Wrong. I probable would eventual know, at a moment when it'd be too late to stop him, and I'd be in trouble up to my dandruff. My pal's master plans were always so simple to see through. Once the scheme was complete. In its early stages, however, I could understand what Luther Vinson was up to about as quickly as I could memorize a textbook on Japanese chemistry.

As I held my end of the string, turning gradually to my left, Soup continued his futile hunt. He looked in buildings, inside barns, and under each and every structure.

But why was he using the string?

Sometimes it would slacken as Soup Vinson retreated to avoid a house here, or a tree there, pausing to yank our lengthy lanyard free of some entangling obstacle. True enough, Soup was circling. But I couldn't, for the life of me, begin to reason out *why*.

"Think," I told myself. "Think!"

I thought.

A piece of string, a football field at the high school, and now Mr. Lem Wheeler's cowshed roof.

Cow + string + football = circle?

Somehow, I knew, these three elements had to unite. They must be totaling up to some weirdo sum in Luther Wesley Vinson's incredible mind. Football. Roof. String. And a one-hundred-yard circle. Soup was indeed making a loop that no one would ever discover.

Ah!

That's why he used string.

To locate something that was a hundred yards from Mr. Wheeler's cowshed, but he didn't know in what direction.

In the distance, I saw Soup poking inside a cowbarn silo. Then, reappearing in less than three seconds, Soup was waving his arms, and jumping up and down in a most happy fashion. He threw his hat into the air. Then turned a clumsy cartwheel.

I felt a joyful tug of the string.

Soup then hollered only one word of discovery.

"Candy!"

Six

"Higher," said Miss Boland.

Soup and I were in town, on our way home from school. Everywhere we looked, we could see blizzards of red hearts.

All sizes.

Hanging here, and dangling there.

A team of three people (two men plus our county nurse) was decorating one of the Main Street lampposts. Needless to say, Miss Boland was giving all of the orders to Mr. Zimmer and Mr. Burlingame.

Miss Boland was on the ground. The two gents, however, were perched on a ladder, hovering close to twenty feet in the air, holding a red heart the size of an extra-large pizza. And also fearfully trying to hold each other as Miss Boland shouted up instructions.

"About an inch higher."

Mr. Zimmer shook his head. "I ain't so sure I can reach up that far. I'll tumble."

"Stand on your toes."

"Can't," said Mr. Burlingame. "Mr. Zimmer's standing on 'em."

Some fresh snow had fallen, about six or seven inches, and the white blanket served as a backdrop for the galaxy of red hearts that now adorned every tree, post, stop sign, and shrub within the village limits.

"Fix it," shouted Miss Boland.

"I'm fixing to fall," complained Mr. Zimmer. "You know I can't abide heights. Even shoes with thick soles make me dizzy."

"Me too," said Mr. Burlingame. "I'm so confounded high up that I'll get myself a nosebleed. I could get the bends."

Soup and I said a howdy to Miss Boland.

"Hey there, boys," she replied. "Well, as you can see, the ladies of our local Triangle Bee Society really kicked in for some shiny red paper and lace. They also constructed most of these hearts. We sure have plenty of good people in this town."

"Everything is starting to look super nice, Miss Boland," said Soup.

"It certain is," I added. "Thanks."

Miss Boland smiled. "Well, I'll be doggoned. You kids are

the first people in town to admit me a thank-you. So permit me to say . . . you're more than welcome." She bent close to us. "To give you the straight of it, I get a heck of a kick out of any breed of holiday celebration."

Miss Boland smiled.

"And," she added, "guess who I got to donate the grand prize for the most creative valentine?"

"Who?" I asked.

"Joe."

"You mean Mr. Joe Spazzatura of Joe's Diner?"

Miss Boland flashed Soup and me a thumbs-up (although inside her mitten) sign. "He of Eat at Joe's fame."

"We got it!" yelped Mr. Zimmer.

"Good," said Miss Boland, "and it looks positively super. So climb down, and we'll fix you gentlemen up with some doughnuts and hot coffee."

"Free?"

"Yup, here it is," she said, "courtesy of Joe's Diner." Miss Boland smiled. "Joe Spazzatura always comes through. He's the poorest person in town. Yet he always gives the most."

Looking around, I could see how a whole bunch of people had laboriously transformed our plain little Vermont town of Learning into a February festival of red and white. Hearts hung everywhere. It made me feel really proud to live in such a nifty hometown. As far as I was concerned, I'd never yearn to reside anywhere else. I would be a citizen of Learning forever.

Miss Boland turned to us.

"Say," she said, "I just might have an extra bit of news."

Soup and I both moved closer to Miss Boland, so we'd be sure to hear her next announcement.

"Joe's offering another prize too."

"Honest?" I asked.

Miss Boland nodded.

"What sort of a prize?" Soup asked.

"Well, according to our friend Joe, it's kind of a special surprise." Miss Boland winked a sly eye. "Would you boys like a little hint as to what it might be?"

"Yes," we said.

Bending, in order to lean closer to our earmuffed ears, our county nurse lowered her voice to a whisper. "Okay, here's your hint. And it's the real inside info."

Holding my breath, I waited.

"Joe," said Miss Boland, "told me that his secret surprise has something to do with a well-known horse."

Soup and I looked at each other, shrugged, and then made a series of wild guesses, naming all of our favorite cowboys.

"Hoot Holler?"

"Buffalo Trill?"

"Hack Smoker?"

"Bighorn Little?"

"Wailon Howell?"

"Tex S. Twangitt?"

As far as Soup and I were concerned, it had to be one of the above gentlemen. All singing cowboys. All played a guitar. And each cowboy we named rode a horse.

Miss Boland smiled. "I won't tell you which one," she said, "but I'll tell you this much." Miss Boland paused. "You sort of came close."

"Which one?" Soup asked her. "Please."

"Oh, no, you don't," she said. "If I squeal, it won't be a surprise. Furthermore, it wouldn't be fair to Joe Spazzatura. Would it?"

"No," we agreed.

"Say," said Miss Boland, "I jotted down a list of details that have to be attended to, prior to our Valentine's Day celebration." Pulling off a mitten with her teeth, Miss Boland produced a folded piece of paper. JOE was printed on it. "How would you two rascals like to do me, and the town, a favor?"

"Just name it," said Soup.

"And we'll do it quick," I said.

"Good," she said. "Then hustle this list of stuff up to Joe at the diner. I know, it's a steep climb up Dugan's Hill, but you'll make it. Joe's my co-chairman on the party committee, so he needs this."

Soup took the note.

"Thanks," said Miss Boland, "and please give my best to Mr. Spazzatura."

Up Dugan's Hill we ran. Well, at first we were running, then trotting, then walking very slowly, until we stopped still for a breather.

"No wonder," said Soup, "that Joe's Diner doesn't get many customers to Eat at Joe's. This is one heck of a climb."

Finally, we made it.

Luckily for us, Joe's Diner was only about halfway up the hill.

A sign on the door said OPEN.

Stomping the snow off our boots, we entered the old beat-up diner that had once been a railroad dining car. Mr. Joe

Spazzatura was there, wearing his usual white apron. Yet the proprietor was the only person we saw inside. There were no customers eating at Joe's. Not even a one.

Nonetheless, Joe greeted us with a friendly smile.

As Soup handed Joe the piece of paper, he said, "Mr. Spazzatura, here's a note."

"For me?"

"Yes," I said, "it's from Miss Boland."

He smiled. "Thank you, boys." He tucked the note into his apron pocket. "I'll read it later, when I can locate my specs."

A little red-and-white valentine was dangling by a frayed string over Joe's cash register. To me, it looked very sad, and lonely, as if Joe had made it himself, yet had no sweetheart to receive it.

Joe saw me looking at his valentine. "Hey," he said, "I made it for my kitten."

"Where is she?" Soup asked.

Joe lifted her up to the counter. "Right here."

We all petted her.

"Say," said Joe, "I got some red paper left over. Not much. But enough to make maybe two more valentines." He eyed Soup, then me. "What do you say? Sometimes, in the stores down in town, a valentine can cost a few pennies more than a boy has to spend."

All I knew was how much I wanted to do something special for Norma Jean Bissell. Making her happy would make me even happier.

So, we constructed three valentines.

Joe's kitten wasn't much help (even though she certain

tried to be) putting her paw in the glue. But, in a way, the little animal was in the spirit of Valentine's Day.

As we cut and pasted, she purred.

"The world loves a kitten," said Joe.

I knew Joe did too.

Seven

"Rob."

Without blinking, or turning around, or taking even one breath, I knew the melodic voice.

Earlier, we had returned the borrowed ball of string to Miss Kelly.

School was over for the day.

I was waiting outside, for Soup, who had been asked by Miss Kelly to remain after recess, for presenting Miss Kelly's wastebasket with a gift. A dead fish. Miss Kelly had also guessed that it had been Soup who had chalked a valentine poem on the blackboard. About *beans* being good for your heart.

Now, however, I turned to face the someone who had just spoken my name. I looked adoringly at Norma Jean Bissell, whom I had secretly named . . . Norma Jean Whistle.

She knew I liked her. On her birthday I'd given her a present, an old shoebox, lined with grass and mud, containing my collection of dead bugs.

There she stood, just outside our school's only door, clothed in winter woolens, yet smiling a sparkle of springtime. She was April in February.

My heart did not leap.

It pole-vaulted.

Mustering all of my courage, and then swallowing the limpy lump of cowardice in my throat as a soda straw would try to gulp a cabbage, I spoke to her.

"Hi."

She advanced a confident step.

Hoping that Norma Jean would not hear my knees that were now chattering together like a pair of false teeth, I bravely held my turf.

No girl would frighten Robert Newton Peck!

Except this one.

"Rob," she said again, saying my name as it was intended to be heard, a Rob that was three fifths of *throb*. "We're having a party this afternoon. But it won't be just for girls. Boys are invited too. The nice ones. Like *you*."

"Oh?" I gulped.

"It isn't exactly a Valentine party, because that's about a week away. It's just an excuse to meet the new family who moved in next door to us." Norma Jean paused to take a deep breath of wintery air. "So, would you like to come to our party, Rob?"

"Uh . . . sure."

Norma Jean smiled. "And bring Soup," she said. "Because we already have enough girls, and almost *any* extra boy we can scare up will be welcome . . . *even your pal.*"

My day flew by.

Norma Jean Bissell had scheduled her social for after school, midafternoon, a time to allow the party guests to hightail home in time for five o'clock chores. So, at three o'clock, Soup and I arrived at the Bissell residence. More than a minute tardy as it had taken considerable convincing to induce Soup to come.

He kept insisting that all of us boys should be paid a fee to attend. In advance.

"At least," he told me, "a dime each."

Even as I knocked, I could hear that Norma Jean's party was already in gear. But as our hostess opened the door to smile at us, all I could hear was female voices. My gullet constricted. Was this a warning? DON'T GO IN. What if the party was . . . *all girls*?

But as Soup and I were yanked inside by Norma Jean, I could spot a few boys. All three of them were quiet. Their faces seemed too frightened to utter even a word. Soup and I hurriedly dashed to join the other boys, seeking the safety of our humble herd.

"They sandbagged us," said Soup. "There's at least two or three times as many girls as guys."

I counted.

Eleven girls. It sounded like thirty.

Here, cowering beyond the dining room table, there were now only five of us boys. There were eleven girls. Maybe even twelve. And six more girls came gushing and giggling and gurgling through the front door, ushered in by Mrs. Bissell.

"We're surrounded," I told Soup.

Sorrowfully he nodded in agreement.

"Rob," I heard Norma Jean's voice sing out, a summons to face my unknown fate.

Reacting, I cracked my knee on the table and it smarted like Holy Heck.

"Are you coming too?" I asked Soup.

"She wants *you*. Not me."

"Rob, I *need* you," insisted Norma Jean, "to meet our new neighbors. They just came in the kitchen door. Now *be polite* as they're only here for a week."

"Okay," I surrendered.

I met the new kids. Politely.

Two girls, both about Norma Jean's age or perhaps a year older, and their brother. And I mean *big* brother.

"Howdy there, little ol' pardner," he boomed to me, offering an open hand one size larger than an outfielder's glove. "Oxide is my name. Oxide Heartburn, but my friends back home in Texas just sort of usual up'n call me Ox."

"Hi," I said, hearing the brittle bones of my right hand being rearranged inside his, "I'm pleased to meet you." I tried not to wince.

"And," said Norma Jean, "these two girls are his sisters.

Twin sisters. I've never met any twins before, and here they are."

"I'm Quickie," said one of the Heartburn girls.

"And I'm Trickie," said her twin.

Looking at Quickie and then at Trickie, already I couldn't tell which was which. They were twins all right. I wondered how *they* could tell themselves apart.

"Quickie and Trickie Heartburn," cooed Norma Jean. "Isn't that cute?"

"Mmm," I mumbled.

Then all the girls graciously assisted Mrs. Bissell in pushing (or dragging) the other four boys, one by one, from beyond the dining room table for proper introductions. Even though Soup, in futile desperation, was stubbornly clinging to a table leg, one corner of a large rug (under which he had tried to hide), and a dog.

A moment earlier, I'd met the Heartburn twins, and had found them about as interesting as bookends. Or maybe andirons.

Then something happened.

Something weird.

"Ladies," said Mrs. Bissell, locking Soup's head in a nifty half nelson, "allow me to present . . . *stop that kicking* . . . Luther Vinson. And this young gentleman is their brother, Oxide."

While good old Ox was pumping (make that pulverizing) Soup Vinson's hand, I happened to notice Soup's face. He wasn't even flinching. Instead of looking at big Ox, he was gazing at Quickie and Trickie, his eyelids at half-mast. His expression was not unlike that of a sick toad. Or a dead one.

Once the introductions were over, Mrs. Bissell went wad-dling off, disappearing into the kitchen, refreshment bound.

"Let's play a game," said Norma Jean.

While I suggested Crack the Whip, Rolly Magraw men-tioned Indian Wrassling, and Hugh Filbert came up with Red Rover. Soup said nothing. His symptoms hadn't changed. No improvement. He just stared at the twins.

"You sick?" I asked him, checking inside his collar for some sign of a rash.

No answer.

"We know a gorgeous game," said Quickie.

"We learned our little ol' game away down yonder," said Trickie, "in itty-bitty Texas."

"What's the game called?" asked Norma Jean.

"Smooch," said the twins.

All the girls tittered their immediate approval.

"I don't like it," Soup whispered.

In less than a minute, each boy and every girl had been assigned a number. Boys were odd. Girls were even. I was *one* and Soup was given *three*.

"We'll start," the twins volunteered. And quicker than a couple of Texas jackrabbits, they sprang from the room, hid behind the parlor piano (or so it seemed), and hollered out a number:

"Three!!!"

I nudged Soup. "Hey . . . that's *you*."

"I'm not going," he hissed.

Soup went.

But reluctantly, and only after Quickie and Trickie re-turned to haul him away, yelping in protest. He was gone for a full five minutes. During that period, I could still hear him screaming, but his cries were muffled, and grew weaker, fainter, and nonexistent.

Upon returning, his gait seemed unsteady, his knees jacked, and the pupils of his eyes were spinning in opposite circles.

Soup's complexion was whiter than a flag of surrender. But, oddly enough, his lips were crimson. Warpaint red. Like mashed cherries. Then, very slowly, the bewildered look on his face blossomed into a feeble smile. He looked almost happy.

"Baseball," he said, "is no longer my favorite sport."

Eight

Norma Jean's party was a base hit.

By that, I mean that everything played along smoothly, until Norma Jean called out my Smooch number, at her first turn at bat. Or whatever the girls called it.

"One," I heard her distant voice yoo-hooing.

"What'll happen to me?" I asked Soup.

"You won't believe it," he answered in a feeble tone, his eyeballs still rotating. "Rob . . . be prepared, and don't be scared. It only hurts at first."

I wondered if he'd meant *first base.*

Bracing myself, I walked manfully out of the room.

Behind me, the girls were giggling, and the boys were trembling; yet I tried to stride forward like a brave soldier about to face enemy gunfire. My brain was still wondering what kind of a game Smooch really was. Or how it was played. All I knew so far was that Soup was *three*, and he'd gotten mussed up (maybe messed up) something fearful.

Quickie and Trickie had ganged up on him.

Unsteadily I paused.

Was there a chance that Norma Jean Bissell would gang up on *me*? Would the spotless name of Rob Peck be tarnished by fact, or rumor? Could a low-voltage town spawn a high-voltage girl?

Fate would decide.

Entering the parlor, I spotted Norma Jean Bissell, and instantly suspected (from the beckoning gleam in her eyes) that Smooch had little or nothing in common with baseball. Infield or outfield.

We boys talked about baseball a lot.

Never about Smooch, or anything at all like it, figuring that someday the girls would explain the rudiments, step by step. Up until this moment, however, no girl had even hinted that Smooch was a party game, like Pin the Tail on the Donkey, or Tag.

So, I approached Norma Jean with extreme caution, to face whatever lay in store.

Or run away.

Mrs. Bissell, I was thinking, should have briefed all of us boys in private. Perhaps handed out a little book of rules, entitled *Dos and Don'ts of Mastering Championship*

Smooch. If not that, maybe a handy pocket pamphlet . . . *Smooching for the Beginner.*

"Hi there, handsome," whispered Norma Jean to the beginner.

Her voice may have been satiny, yet her grip on my shirt was demanding, as I was suddenly pulled behind the piano. It was a large brown upright, placed diagonally in a corner. If Smooch required a lot of territory (like a baseball diamond), Norma Jean had chosen a skimpy location. Where we now stood, very close together, there was hardly a foot of extra game space. Barely room for a bunt.

And no scoreboard.

In the past, at parties, a lot of girls had managed to beat me at a whole bunch of tests and contests, ranging from Horseshoes to Hopscotch.

My mother, however, often allowed me to win, at checkers, and ditto for Aunt Carrie.

"Hello Rob," said Norma Jean.

Her softening voice puzzled me. At baseball games, people yell a lot, and holler things like "Kill the umpire!" or "He was safe by a mile!" There was also popcorn and hot dogs and relish and mustard and ketchup and cotton candy and bubble gum and soda pop . . . until a kid finally threw up, and was carried home.

Why was Norma Jean whispering? And if I became ill, would Mrs. Bissell have to carry me home?

Right now, here, an inch away from Norma Jean Bissell, I realized that I hadn't gobbled even one single party treat. Not as much as a peanut half. Yet my stomach seemed to be trying to communicate, as though wanting to tell me something, or warn me about certain digestive disorders.

"Okay," sighed Norma Jean.

"Okay?" I asked.

"Yes," she said quietly, "do it."

Do it?

I was willing to try anything once, including when I attempted to bat lefty, instead of righty. Hitting left is no cinch.

"I'm . . . not a . . . really not a . . ."

"Not a what?" asked Norma Jean Bissell.

"I'm not a lefty."

"A . . . a *whaty*?"

"You know," I quickly explained. Girls are so thick-witted about some things that you have to go really slow whenever you try to clarify anything in detail. "I'm . . . uh . . . not left-handed."

Norma Jean flinched. "And what's *that* supposed to mean?"

"Well . . . uh . . . I'm a righty. If I was a lefty, maybe I'd play first. But seeing as I'm born the way I am, I won't get to first base."

"Not," said Norma Jean, "at the speed *you're* going."

"I've never played before."

"No," said Norma Jean Bissell, "kidding."

I nodded.

"Neither has Soup," I said, feeling my underwear begin to itch. "Have you ever noticed," I asked her, "that some people are better, at a certain kind of game, than others?"

"Oh," said Norma Jean, "have I ever!"

She seemed to be aware that I was scratching.

"What's wrong?"

"I can't tell you," I said.

This was true.

I wouldn't be a very nice boy, were I to tell girls that my winter underwear was the itchy kind; and, whenever I got nervous, it could just about tickle me crazy. In several places. One place was behind a piano. Winter long johns, I was convinced, come fully equipped. Lice included.

"It makes you want to . . . to . . ."

"Call another number," Norma Jean said. "Rob, we've been standing here, where nobody can see us, for over a minute. Maybe two minutes."

"How long does . . . uh . . . Smooch last?"

"If handled properly," she said, "a lifetime."

"Oh."

"But *you* have to start it," she said. "That's what a boy is supposed to do. A girl doesn't."

"What does a *girl* do?"

"Well," whispered Norma Jean Bissell, as her face seemed to be leaning toward mine, "sometimes a girl closes her eyes, and perhaps makes tiny little noises . . . like a kitten."

I smiled. "Mr. Joe Spazzatura . . . you know, up at the Eat at Joe's diner on Dugan's Hill . . . well, he's got himself a new kitten. She can purr like you wouldn't believe."

"So can I," she said.

"Whenever you touch her."

"You're catching on," said Norma Jean. "Does the kitten purr whenever she's kissed?"

Norma Jean's lips seemed to be directly in front of mine.

Closer. Closer. This wasn't resembling anything like base-ball. Not a bit. Nor was it similar to any of the party games I'd ever played. Not knowing exactly what to do, I did the next best thing.

I swallowed.

Her eyes closed. "Please do it."

Having absolutely no idea what Norma Jean Bissell wanted me to do, I closed *my* eyes too. Out of fright. Then, unable to keep my balance very steady, I leaned forward. My lips accidentally met hers.

It wasn't like a bump.

Bumps feel hard. This didn't.

Surprisingly, it wasn't in the least repulsive. Eyes closed, I moved my lips to hers, and stayed. That was when I felt Norma Jean's fingers (left hand on one side and right hand on the other) begin to walk slowly up my shirt. Up, and up, all the way until her arms were around my neck.

I didn't know what to do with *my* hands. Lefty or righty. So, for balance, I just sort of snaked 'em around her waist-line, and held on tight, to prevent my becoming dizzy and then falling against her piano.

Then it hit me!

WHAMBO.

This was a whole different game! Yet we were playing it. Norma Jean Bissell and I, and I didn't even give a hoot whether I was winning, or losing. It seemed like a tie ball game. Even though I'd never been too good at games, I seemed to be winning. At least I felt like a winner. Better than that.

Like a champion!

"Wow," I remarked at last, when the need for breathing made me quit doing all the good stuff, "I'd rather do that than play baseball."

Norma Jean didn't say anything.

She just purred.

So did I.

Norma Jean Bissell must have been eating chocolate just before calling my number. I could taste it. Boy! Life really is a Hershey's Kiss.

On the way home, still in some strange sort of a coma, I confessed to Soup Vinson that I was maybe (well, sort of) in love.

Soup sighed. "That goes double for me."

Nine

It was Saturday.

Chores were over, so Soup Vinson and I were headed for Learning. I hoped that we weren't also heading for trouble.

Once in town, Soup stopped to point.

"Look," he said.

I looked. Blinking, I saw little or nothing, except for the △ B sign beside the door of the local chapter of the Triangle Bee Society. It was some sort of a civic club for the ladies of Learning.

"Notice anything new, Rob?"

"No."

"Look again."

Again I looked.

"Okay," I said with a sigh, "I give up. What in the heck were you pointing at?"

"The Triangle Bee Society," said Soup, taking a step in its direction, "has a new sign, as any fool can plainly see. I saw it right away quick."

"So what?"

He clapped me upon the shoulder with a hale and hearty mitten. "It just came to me, Rob. A sign is exactly what you and I are sorely in need of. But not just any old sign."

I faced him.

"*No*," I said, "we're not stealing their new sign."

Soup grinned.

"No," he agreed, "we are not."

I breathed easier.

"However," he said, "a new sign tells us something, Robert, old top. In fact, their new sign is a harbinger of an exciting event to come."

"It is?"

Soup nodded. "A new sign," he said, "means that we ought to go around to the back and check out a possibility."

Scooting up a narrow alley, we went to the rear of the Triangle Bee Society. "Behold!" said Soup. "What did I tell you? There it is, sitting right handy and in plain sight."

Soup was right. Leaning against a wall was their *old* sign. It seemed somewhat larger than the shiny new $\triangle B$ that now adorned the front entrance. "I suspected it all along," said Soup, racing to the familiar two symbols.

"Suspected what?"

"Nobody," said Soup, "in the entire state of Vermont can ever throw anything away."

What my pal was saying was true. Because time and time again, my mother would plop a plateful of food in front of me, stuff that almost screamed "unidentified frying objects," and then announce that, unless I ate, she would be forced to perform that most dreaded of unpardonable acts, described in seven sorrowful words:

"Unless you eat it," Mama would plead in a plaintive voice, *"I'll only have to throw it out."*

"And," Soup continued to say, "it's plain as daylight that the Triangle Bee ladies no longer have a use for their former sign. That's why it's back here. It's junk."

My mind was working as well as his.

"So," I said, "you're planning to take it."

Soup nodded.

"But," he said quickly, "in order to ease your worry, we don't intend to keep it. Neither will we use it for ourselves."

"What'll we use it for?"

Soup lifted up the red triangle, grunted, and quickly set it down. "A bit bulkier than I first imagined," he said. "But, to answer your question, this discarded sign is just what we need, Rob." Soup jumped up and down. "Can't you see?"

"No," I confessed.

"Remember what we found a hundred yards from Mr. Lem Wheeler's cowshed, with the help of Miss Kelly's ball of string?"

I remembered. "Yes, a pair of giant candy canes painted red white red white red white, and so on."

"But," said Soup with a sly wink, "they're not *really* candy canes, are they?"

I shook my head. They weren't.

They were toboggans.

"Thus," said my pal, "if you take those two long

Christmasy objects, add an old Triangle Bee Society sign, and top it all off with the core of our creation . . . which has a lot to do with Joe's new refrigerator . . . what do you final come up with?"

Soup waited while I thought.

This was typical. Because the more Luther Wesley Vinson explained, the more confusing it all became.

"Give me a hint," I said.

Soup was down on one knee in the snow, peeking behind the other red symbol, the large red B. He seemed to be satisfied by what he saw.

"Okay," he said, "we're going to create a most unusual valentine, make a sudden and dramatic entrance into town and impress the girls we love . . . Quickie and Trickie and Norma Jean . . . by winning the grand prize that Joe's Diner offered."

"Is that all?"

"No, not quite," said Soup with a chuckle.

"There's more?"

"We are going to have *fun* besides."

"Will we get in trouble?"

Soup frowned. "Of course not." As his face returned to its usual cheer, he added, "But we can't do all this by ourselves. We need a palooka."

"A what?"

"You know. In bank-robbing movies, when they collect a gang to pull a *bank job*, and start planning to rob it, there's a getaway-car driver, a safecracker, a mastermind who is usual the boss, a gunman, and a two-fisted pug. *He*," said Soup, "is the *palooka*."

We two left the back alley behind the Triangle Bee Society building and returned to Main Street. More hearts seemed to be tacked up. Our little town of Learning was festively festooned.

"Wow," said Soup, glancing in one direction and then another, "Learning's in love."

I agreed.

Secretly, I was wondering what kind of candy I might include in my valentine for Norma Jean Bissell. Nothing expensive like chocolates. But maybe a gumdrop or a slightly mashed jelly bean.

We strolled along the street.

"Rob," asked Soup, "which one is it?"

"Which one is what?"

"Which cowboy's horse?"

"Hoot Holler," I guessed.

"Nope," said Soup, "it'll be Buffalo Trill."

"Good old Mr. Spazzatura," I said, "certain deserves a lot of credit, for offering the prizes."

"He sure does," Soup agreed. "What a guy."

Outside the 5-and-10 store, we saw Miss Boland pausing to look at a large valentine in the window. We said hello to her.

Miss Boland smiled. "My," she said, "all these red valentines, everywhere we look. It even cranks up *my* old heart to romance speed."

She left, humming a love song.

Soup and I ventured inside the store.

All of the pretty valentines were too dearly priced for Soup and me to afford. Some of the fancy ones were marked away up as precious as fifteen cents.

Soup sighed. "Money is a problem."

"It certain is."

"How," asked Soup, "do two penniless boys afford valentines for the three girls they love?"

Ten

Bump!

As Soup and I bolted away from the greeting card racks at the 5-and-10, we should have watched where we were going.

But we didn't. Instead, we crashed into a very large person who was also shopping for a valentine.

"Hey," said Ox. "How y'all good ol' boys?"

Oxide Heartburn was certainly a friendly fellow, and I started liking him. Soup was smiling, so I figured he felt likewise. We picked ourselfs up off the floor.

"Doing some shopping, Ox?" asked Soup.

"Ya'll bet," he said. But then Ox's warm pizza face seemed to sadden into its empty pan. "But doggone-a-shootin' if I can decide which of all them pretty little valentines that I oughta up'n buy for a gal I sorta hanker."

My pal and I glanced at each other. Soup, then looking back at Ox, asked what the girl's name was.

Ox blushed.

"Aw," he said, "I don't reckon I oughta tell." His face drained to sober. "Besides, I don't know her family name at all. Only her first name."

Soup didn't press to learn what the girl's name was. Nor did I. Some matters were too personal for prying.

"I never even yet said a little bitty ol' *howdy* to her," Ox confessed. "On account we never yet been properly introduced."

"Was she at the party?" I asked.

Ox said, "I don't recall."

Pulling off a mitten with his teeth, Soup snapped his fingers. "Say," he said, "maybe I just thought of an idea, Ox, that would help out all of us."

"Like what?" he cautiously asked.

Soup paced back and forth, stopped, snapped his fingers one more time, and launched headlong into an explanation. "Ox," he said, "suppose Rob and I could wangle you a . . . as you say . . . a proper introduction to this girl, the one that tickles your fancy. If we do this big favor for you, would you consider doing likewise for the two of us?"

"Gee," said Ox, "I sure-as-shootin' would."

Soup shot me a wink.

"Good," he said. "So let's go."

"Where?" asked Ox. "We can't go to *her* house. I don't even have a necktie on, or my hair combed proper."

"Steady," said Soup, holding up a restraining hand. "Nobody said anything about taking you to her house." He paused. "What I have in mind," Soup whispered, "is soliciting your assistance for a worthy and noble cause."

"Count me in," said Ox.

"Let's go," said Soup Vinson.

We left the 5-and-10. In less than three minutes, the three of us (Soup and Ox and I) were again behind the Triangle Bee Society headquarters, near their old discarded sign.

"I wonder," said Soup, "should we attempt to haul it all in one trip . . . or two."

"One'd be easier," said Ox.

"It's a heavy load," warned Soup.

Oxide Heartburn grinned a sheepish grin. "Back home in Texas, they called me Ox because I'm so strong."

"That," said Soup, "is what we're counting on."

As my best friend fired me another quick wink, it began to dawn on me exactly what Luther Wesley Vinson had found for us. Our necessary *palooka*. It was Oxide. My brain was racing. Bank job. BANK JOB. Good grief, was Soup Vinson intending to *rob a bank*?

"Soup," I said quickly, "count me out."

His eyebrows raised.

"Rob, old tiger, no one's going to count you out. At least not until you're down."

Shaking my head, I said, "I'm not going to be part of any"—(I whispered)—"*bank job.*"

Soup shrugged. "What a pity. Oh well, I guess we best change our plans. Instead of a bank robbery, we'll just do the nice ladies of the Triangle Bee Society a favor. A good turn."

"Like what?" Ox asked Soup.

"Well," said Soup, "for starters, before we introduce our good friend Ox to the prettiest girl in town . . . whoever she may be . . . we'll perform our good deed for the day and cart these two red hunks of discarded junk to The Dump."

I breathed easier.

"Bend over, Ox," said Soup.

Ox bent to a bow.

"Okay, Robert, lend me a hand and help me lift this triangle onto Ox's mighty withers."

Grunting, straining, we did it.

"Is that heavy?" Soup asked Ox.

"Naw. I can take heavier."

We added the other sign piece, the giant red B, so it lay on the red triangle. Ox's hands hooked around to steady his strange-looking load.

"Where to," he asked us, "to a trash heap?"

"Sort of," Soup said quickly.

With a bit of effort, we managed to point Ox in the general direction. Soup, I noticed, did not select a direct route. His chosen path was one of total obscurity, in shadows, behind buildings and along the seldom-trod byways of town. We headed up Dugan's Hill.

"Hey," grunted Ox, from beneath his burden, "I don't seem to be on the flat any longer. Are you guys on level ground?"

"We," said Soup, "are rarely on the level."

"How much farther? This here load's growing a lot heavier than when I started this trip."

"We're almost there," said Soup. "Only another hundred yards to go. If you ever played football, Ox, just think of it as sort of scoring a very long touchdown. You'll be the hero of the day."

"I will?"

"Right," said Soup.

Ox was grunting up the hill, under his load, his labored steps becoming shorter and shorter.

"We need a whip," said Soup, "or a stronger palooka. Or a *horse*. Say, we should've borrowed that old white horse at Mr. Spazzatura's."

"You mean Black Thunder?"

Soup shrugged. "Well, it's too late now."

We final made it to the top. Even though it was a nippy February day in Vermont, Ox already broke a sweat. A cold sweat, I hoped. Or at least a cool one.

Then we went to The Dump, located the gigantic carton that had once housed Joe's new secondhand refrigerator, and allowed our mighty friend Ox to move it. After that, the three of us headed toward Lem Wheeler's cowshed, and beyond, to the exact spot where Soup had jumped up and down, tossed his wool hat into the air, and hollered, "Candy!"

We located Soup's discovery.

A double one, painted (alternately in red and white) to appear as peppermint candy canes. They were really a pair of very long toboggans. In shoddy condition.

Ox hauled one.

Soup and I lugged the other.

Ox did it in a breeze, but Soup and I were almost wiped out by fatigue. It certain was handy to have a palooka like Oxide Heartburn around, even if we weren't pulling a bank heist.

"Okay," said our palooka pal at last, "you fellows've got all this useless stuff together . . . I won't ask for why . . . so now are you going to introduce me to the young lady who I know is going to be just my type? Oh boy, I can't wait to meet her."

Soup nodded.

"Sure thing, Ox, old buddy. A deal is a deal. Rob and I know every gal in town, don't we, tiger?"

"We sure do," I said. "Here in Learning, just about everybody knows just about everybody else."

"How come?" Ox asked us.

"Because," said Soup, "we're all worth knowing."

Ox smiled a shy smile.

"However," said Soup, "*you* have to give us a start, a clue. We figure she's about your age, or ours, so all you supply is her first name. Robert Peck and Soup Vinson will fill in the important details."

"Right," I said. "Now what's the first name of this special girl who has captured your fancy?"

Ox blushed oxblood.

"Janice."

Eleven

It had to happen.

Soup, enrapt with the fevers and fervors of love, found a jackknife. Used, but in a surprising mint condition, and sharper than Miss Kelly's eyesight when her back was turned.

"What'll I carve?" he asked me.

I shrugged. "Well, you could always carve your initials, L.W.V., on your desk. That, of course, might not go over so big with our teacher."

Soup Vinson's face lit up.

"I got it. I'll carve a heart. What could be more fitting, seeing as Valentine's Day is nigh upon us?"

This he did.

Luther Wesley Vinson carve a small heart? No, not he. Soup cut a very large one into the wood of the pigsty owned by Mr. Adkin Skudblister, the oldest member of Learning's Town Council. He was presumed to be at least eighty years of age. Some claimed he'd fought in the Civil War. Others said it was The Crusades. Yet there, for all eyes to see, hung a heart the size of an archery target; and inside it, a personal inscription by the carver to his sweetheart:

L.W.V. loves
Miss Heartburn

"This," Soup insisted, "will cover all bases, because both Quickie and Trickie are truly the Miss Heartburn. Get it?"

We were on Main Street.

"Look who's coming," I said.

Soup looked, and then smiled. "Ah," he said, "as we now speak, here comes one of the Heartburn twins."

"But which one?" I asked.

"Please don't confuse me with the facts," Soup told me. "Love isn't factual. It's fun." He grinned. "Watch how deftly I handle my problem of names."

She approached us. All smiles.

"Hi Chickie," said Soup.

I had to give Luther Wesley Vinson credit. He could dodge a elephant in a phone booth. Or a bullet inside a gun barrel.

Quickie (or perhaps it was Trickie) looked at Soup and gave him a wide Texas smile. And then told him how pleased she was at seeing how tastefully he had carved the heart at the pigsty. But then asked Soup a question. "Luther, was that heart for me, love dove, or was it for Trickie?"

"For you, Quickie," said Soup, "for *you*."

She skipped away.

Later, we met her again. (So I thought.) This time, however, she wasn't smiling. "Luther, was that heart you carved for *me*, or for Quickie?"

"For *you*, Trickie."

She left, dancing happy steps, and singing a cheerful tune.

"Wow," said Soup, "those Heartburn twins are both prettier than strawberry jam on a hot biscuit."

Turning to Soup, I said, "The jam, that you're so hungry for, may not be on the biscuit you're fixing to eat. In fact, instead of the jam in you, you'll be in a jam."

Soup laughed.

"Or," I added, "in the pigsty."

"Nonsense," said Soup, "what could possible go wrong?"

I answered him. "Double trouble."

Closing his eyes, Soup inhaled a deep breath of winter, then exhaled with a sigh. "Ah," he said, "it's in the air."

"Mr. Skudblister's pigsty?"

"No. Rob, old sport, what I smell is the February fragrance of frolic and festivity." He turned to face me. "So, let's go."

"Go where?"

Soup said, "To the most inspirational place in town, a quiet haven where we so often visit, to seek and then to find creativity."

We went to The Dump.

"Valentine's Day is tomorrow," said Soup, "and we have three girls to impress, Quickie and Trickie and Chickie. Sorry, I meant Norma Jean. So let's hustle up what we need to assemble our prizewinning valentine."

"Okay."

"Look for wire, Rob. Or some old rope that's not too aged that it'll pop. Did you bring the hammer?"

"Yes." I held it up for Soup to see.

"Good, stout fellow. Pry some old nails out of those dirty boards and then bang 'em straight." Soup, meanwhile, was measuring the long side of Mr. Joe Spazzatura's discarded refrigerator crate. "Perfect," he announced, "as long as it doesn't zoom too fast."

I looked up from an unbent nail.

"Too fast?"

Soup grinned. "Just a figure of speech. I was referring more to our constructional progress than I was to eventual downhill acceleration."

His last remark did little (try *nothing*) to steady my already apprehensive nervous system. I smelled disaster; to me, it stunk worse than The Dump.

A thought struck.

"Soup, is that big empty refrigerator box going to sit on the two candy-cane toboggans . . . and be some kind of a vehicle?"

"Sort of."

"I don't like the idea."

"Fear not. There's a plan cooking in my brain that can't miss. You'll soon see," said Soup.

"What kind of a plan is it?"

"A master plan." Soup, atop a mound of debris and garbage, stretched both of his mittens skyward. "The twin toboggans, which I shall name Quickie and Trickie, will carry our big box downhill, and into town. Once there, it will serve to contain all of the valentine cards that people are giving to other people."

"Oh," I said. But then another thought crossed my mind. "What are we using the red triangle and B for?"

"That," said Soup, "is our surprise."

Whenever my pal used that particular term, the *surprise* was usual some kind of a crashing disaster. But, I then decided, as my hammer unwarped another bent nail, nothing could go wrong. Or could it? Being a partner in one of Soup's insanities often flirted with failure. Add to that, the twins might cut Soup in half, as he merrily slid down the razor blade of romance.

Soup unfolded some strange sort of a blueprint, one that he obviously had carefully drawn, and was now studying it.

"Ah," he said, "that'll do it."

"Do what?"

Soup smiled. "Create our valentine. Rob, help me lug that big red triangle closer to the refrigerator crate. No! Hold it. First we mount the crate on the two candy-cane toboggans. Then nail it all together."

This we did.

Much to my amazement, it looked like a giant box sled on two long wooden runners with upturned toes.

"Now," said Soup, "we have Eat at Joe's on one side, and our genius about to decorate the other. A symphony of red and white."

"I don't get it."

"You will. Gimme a hand. First we nail the triangle to the side of the crate." We lifted it into place. "No, not like that, Rob. Our triangle has to be positioned with a *flat edge up* and *one point down*."

"Like your blueprint?"

"Exactly."

We nailed the big red triangle in place and according to Soup Vinson's design.

"I don't get it, Soup. It's just a red triangle."

"Only for now," Soup said. "In construction, you have to have foresight, not to see *what is* but rather to envision eventually *what shall be*."

"Okay," I said, "let's do it."

We did it. The second step was harder, and heavier, because we had to grunt the large red B above the triangle.

"Flat side to flat side," Soup commanded. "We put the B on sideways, flat part down and bumps up."

"All this is going to look like," I groaned, straining, while Soup pounded in nail after nail, "is a B and a triangle."

We were finished, at last.

Then we stepped back to admire our genius, or our lunacy. However, much to my dismay, the B atop the triangle became one entity, one magnificent and artistic object.

A big shiny red heart!

Twelve

It snowed.

Oh, it snowed very hard on the thirteenth day of February, the day before Valentine's Day. The snowflakes were light and dry.

As Soup and I were walking down Dugan's Hill, we turned our coat collars up. The weather had turned breezy. A stiff northern wind caused the feathery snow to blow into drifts, some of them almost mounting to the height of a second-story window.

Halfway down the long, steep hill, we came to Joe's Diner & Diesel Fuel Stop. The big sign, <u>Eat at Joe's</u>, looked a bit shabby.

"Hey," said Soup, "let's stop in and say a friendly howdy to our old friend, Mr. Joe Spazzatura."

"Good idea."

In we went.

Joe, in his white apron, was behind the long counter, serving hot meals to (I counted) seven customers. All lumberjacks. It made me happy to see that Mr. Spazzatura was handling some trade.

Stomping the snow off our boots, Soup and I looked up to see Mr. Joe Spazzatura's welcoming smile.

"Hello boys."

We petted his little kitten for a while. After the customers paid, and left, Joe gave Soup and me a free cookie. One each.

We thanked him.

Munching my chocolate-chipper, I reread the words printed on the little sign on Joe's wall:

A MAN TAKES TO HEAVEN ONLY WHAT
HE GIVES AWAY ON EARTH.

It made me wonder if someday, after I was all grown up and married (I hoped) to Norma Jean Peck, I'd own a diner like Joe's. Rob's Diner. If so, I'd try to be nice like Joe Spazzatura, and treat all the kids to cookies.

And some milk to kittens.

It was certain a shame that the lead mill had closed. Mr.

Spazzatura deserved to have a lot of customers, not just a few. Joe's Diner, however, was too distant from the center of town; plus the fact that it was located over halfway up a very steep climb.

Dugan's Hill.

It was named, so local legend maintained, after a gentleman named Dugan who tried to ski down the hill. And he actual did. He never fell. He stopped! Mr. Dugan, unluckily, stopped very abruptly when he skied, at a very high speed, into the brick wall of Rooker's Garage. The bricks never moved. And, after the crash, Mr. Dugan never moved either.

"Say," said Joe, "in the back room, in the shed next to my kitchen, I got all the valentines stored. That's because our Post Office didn't have any storage space, so Miss Boland had the mail truck haul 'em up here. She didn't want any valentines delivered until tomorrow." He sighed. "She's a incharge."

"Well," said Soup, "whatever Miss Boland wants, she usual gets. That's because she does so much good for Learning."

"Right," I agreed. "I'd hate to see our town without her." Joe nodded.

"Ah yes," he said softly, "we have plenty of good people here in Learning. I was born in Italy, as you know, and still have some relatives there. Napoli is my birthplace, but Vermont holds my heart."

I noticed some cigarette butts, burnt matches, a gum wrapper, and a couple of paper napkins on the floor. Beneath the stools where the lumbermen had eaten.

Grabbing a broom, I swept the floor for Joe; and Soup, with a dustpan, helped me tidy up.

Mr. Spazzatura waved a thank-you.

After we left, Soup and I walked down the hill and into town, to see what merriment the afternoon would bring. I was hoping to see Norma Jean Bissell shopping with her mother. Or, better yet, alone.

Thinking about her, I sighed.

Soup sighed *twice*.

Looking around, I had to admit that Miss Boland (and her team of eager elves) had performed a nifty job at decorating all of Learning. Even the fire hydrants were entwined with white bunting, to trim their normal red.

A dog came along, and looked confused.

But then he spotted another dog, a female, and the two of them went racing off in the snow together, happily, as if life was all love.

Soup managed to greet one of the Heartburn twins with a "Hi Chickie." I didn't know which one it was. Neither did Soup. I wondered if the girl knew.

I also questioned what Soup Vinson intended to do, or say, if he happened to meet *both* Quickie and Trickie.

"Hey," said Soup, "look at that."

I looked.

Strolling along Main Street, holding hands beneath the reds and whites of a hundred hearts of all sizes, were Oxide Heartburn and Janice Riker. It made me wonder if they were, accidentally or intentionally, cracking each other's knuckles. Janice was rarely happy without cracking some-thing, or somebody.

"Aw," said Soup, gazing at Janice and Ox, "now isn't that sweet. It makes me glad we introduced them."

"Janice is actual smiling," I said in disbelief.

"Ox," said Soup, "ought to get a medal. For valor."

I agreed.

From where we stood, it appeared as though Oxide was about to kiss Janice. That, I was imagining, took guts.

"Soup," I asked, "if you were as big and as strong as Oxide Heartburn, would you dare to kiss Janice Riker?"

"Not," he said, "without a catcher's mask."

As Soup and I moved along the street, a little closer to Ox and his beloved, it sudden seemed to me that Janice wasn't looking her usual ugly. In fact, she almost looked pretty. Not, mind you, as pretty as Norma Jean Bissell.

"It just goes to show," I said to Soup, "that love can really improve people."

Soup nodded. "I have to admit," he said, "that Janice Riker's temper has been . . . well, to coin a phrase, tempered. She's a lot nicer."

I assented. "However," I said, "let's avoid Janice, even though she hasn't slugged me in nearly a week."

After ducking through the 5-and-10, Harry's Hardware, the furniture store, the bank, the United States Post Office, the corner drugstore, and our local Pay-as-you-go Funeral Parlor, my pal and I decided that Janice (just in case she became unloving) wouldn't find us.

We didn't see her, or Oxide.

But we did see Miss Kelly, walking along Main Street, admiring all of the hearty decorations.

"Miss Kelly!" we both yelled.

"What are *you* doing here?" I asked.

For some reason, she laughed. "Children," she said, "never expect to see me anywhere but behind my desk, at school. I do move, you know." To illustrate, she angularly bent up her arm, like a robot.

"Say," said Soup, "that's pretty agile."

"My," she said, "our decorations are really lovely." She sighed. "It brings back the times when I was a young girl."

"Did they have Valentine's Day way back in those days?" I asked her.

"Yes. But, of course, we couldn't hang our valentines outdoors."

"Why not?" Soup wanted to know.

"Because," Miss Kelly whispered, "they would have all been eaten by the dinosaurs."

She walked on, still chuckling.

We watched her go, bracing herself against the wind, bundled by a coat that had been battered by too many winters.

"I wonder," said Soup, "if Miss Kelly ever had a boyfriend."

That night, I asked Mama if she'd ever heard, years ago, that Miss Kelly had a sweetheart. To my surprise my mother said yes, and Aunt Carrie agreed. Both of them remembered a fine young man whose name was Ed Nulty. He and Miss Kelly were to be married. But then he was killed at a place named France, in the World War.

That night, on the thirteenth of February, I mentioned

Miss Kelly in my prayers, as I always did. On my knees. But on this night I added one more name to my God Bless list.

A soldier named Edward Nulty.

Thirteen

It final come.

The calendar read February 14.

"It's here at last," said Soup Vinson.

"Yup," I agreed, "and today we present our special valentine box to the entire town, win the prize, and also win the hearts of our favorite girls."

"All three of them," Soup said.

Earlier, in fact for days, both Miss Boland and Mr. Joe Spazzatura had been busily collecting all the valentines that local people (young and old) were giving one another. The valentines had been stored at the diner in gray sacks that Joe had borrowed from the Learning Post Office. Bag upon bag after bag.

"I got no more room," Joe told us.

So, Soup and I, with the help of our friendly neighborhood palooka, Oxide Heartburn, hauled the bags of valentines out of Joe's Diner. We dragged them uphill to our hiding place near The Dump, stowing the valentines in our large box, formerly Joe's refrigerator crate. On one side of the crate, it said Eat at Joe's. On the other was our giant heart, made from a red triangle and a red letter.

But, as luck would have it, the Post Office informed us that it needed the bags back, and pronto. So we emptied out the valentines loosely into one big pile, inside our crate.

Ox helped us slide our ponderous crate-on-runners so it pointed down Dugan's Hill and directly into Learning. It was positioned, however, safely on a flat area.

"A piece of cake," said Soup. "Our crate will glide into town. Then the judges, Miss Kelly and Miss Boland, and Joe, can pass out the valentines and award us first prize. Whereby," he added, "the two of us shall be amply greeted by our three sweethearts . . . Quickie and Trickie and Norma Jean."

"Simple," I said.

"My plan?"

"No," I told him. "*You're* simple."

"Why?"

"How does a great big crate," I asked Soup, "manage to steer itself correctly, going all the way down Dugan's Hill? We're even a quarter of a mile above Joe's Diner."

Soup grinned.

There we stood, away up the hill above town, inside our crate, knee-deep in undelivered valentines in little white envelopes. It seemed too complex a project. We could fail, and humiliate our friend Joe. What we wanted to do was give Joe's Diner some extra publicity.

"Here's how we steer it," said Soup. "You in front, and me in the back."

My throat tightened. "Not inside."

"Yes."

"We're in *here*, sliding this monster down that hill, and we can't even see where we're going?"

"Right. Because, old top, I've had the foresight to borrow something from Mr. Clarkson Roodermyer's boathouse."

"Borrow what? I don't know what you've taken now, but I hope it's a life preserver."

Diving into the white pile of envelopes, Soup searched frantically, then emerged, holding a long wooden object.

"This," he said.

"A canoe paddle?"

"Never be up the hill without a paddle." Soup laughed, charmed by his cleverness. "It's our tiller. You'll be stationed up front, as a lookout, and I'll work the paddle back here, in the stern, so to speak, as a *rudder*."

"You're mad," I told Soup. "You are stark naked mad. We never planned to be inside this death trap. All I figured was that we'd push it, and *watch it* slide into town."

Soup wasn't listening.

With his knife, he was busily poking a hole in the rear of the crate just large enough to accommodate the canoe paddle. His so-called rudder.

"How do we *stop* it?"

"Easy," said Soup. "At the bottom of the hill, the grade levels off, and this crate will ease to a stop, as we hit town."

"You're sure?"

"Positive."

"How will we get it started?"

"Ox will push."

"Suppose, with you and me and all these valentines inside, it's too heavy to push?"

"Janice will help push it. Rob, you haven't forgotten how strong Janice is, have you?"

"No," I said, rubbing an ancient bruise.

"Good."

"Where do I stand?"

"Up front, on the valentine pile," Soup informed me. "See where I cut that little window hole?" I saw. "Well, you'll be here inside, with your head poking out through that square hole, and giving me hand signals."

"You mean lefty or righty?"

"No. I mean port or starboard."

"I don't know the difference. In fact," I admitted to Soup,

"I don't guess I even know what either one of those two words mean."

"Neither," said Soup, "do I."

"I don't like it."

"Well, do you want *me* to act as the forward lookout, and *you* remain back here in the stern to manipulate the paddle, to take full responsibility as our helmsman?"

"No, not really."

"Okay, then it's all settled," Soup said with a definite nod. "I told Ox to bring Janice and meet us here. They'll be along any minute."

Soup was right.

They came.

But I soon spotted a different look on the broad and beefy face of Oxide Heartburn. Instead of warm, it was neighborly close to hot.

"Luther," he said, picking Soup up with one hand, to hold him with a horizontally straight arm, "my little twin sisters aren't exactly too happy. And they said it was all your fault."

He shook Soup like a rag doll.

With one hand.

"If my baby sisters are blue," said Oxide, "sometimes it makes me turn very red. Then, when I'm angry, I break stuff." Soup, looking very breakable, turned pale. "Because," said Ox, "I happen to try to be a nice big brother, and I love both of my baby sisters."

Again he shook my pal, and Soup rattled like a gourd full of seeds.

"Quickie and Trickie don't know which one you favor, Luther, and we better find out," Ox said, "and right now."

Bending his arm, Ox brought Soup close to his face, eye to eye. Soup's boots dangled in the air, slightly lower than Oxide's belt buckle.

"You see," Ox said, "I love 'em *both.*"

Soup gulped. "So do I."

"Both?" Ox asked.

Soup nodded.

Oxide smiled slowly. "That's real nice," he said in a softer voice. "Nice for you maybe. Not for them." Ox's smile widened. "Sometime soon," he said, "I'm fixing to settle this problem for keeps." He held Soup high in the air. "We'll settle it . . . Texas style!"

He dropped Soup into the snow.

"Until then," Oxide said to Soup, "no hard feelings, son." He held out a hand for Soup to shake.

Soup shook it.

But he was wrong about Ox and Janice. Even together they couldn't push our valentine-loaded crate forward enough to budge it an inch.

"We need power," said Soup.

"What kind of power?" Ox asked.

Soup Vinson grinned. "Horse power."

I held my frozen breath.

"What we need," said Soup, "is a gentle old horse to nudge us to the brink of the hill."

Ox and Janice and I all looked at one another, not trusting ourselves to speak. I would have bet every penny in the

world that they were thinking exactly what I was thinking. The name of an old white horse. The only horse
nearby:

Black Thunder.

"No," I protested. "We'd better not."

"Better not what?" Soup asked.

"Use . . . Black Thunder."

"Good idea, Rob," said Soup. "And remember, *you*
will get all the credit for concocting such an inventive
ploy."

They all nodded, the cowards.

"Janice," said Soup, "go steal your mother's clothesline, or
somebody else's, and be back here in ten minutes." She left.
"Ox, run down to Henry's Livery Stable and borrow a harness." He left. "Rob, all that's left for you to tackle, so it
seems, is to get yourself going . . . and bring back Black
Thunder."

"Me?"

"He's your idea. You know where he is, at Joe's place,
behind the diner."

Why I did it, I'll never understand. Nor will I begin to
savvy *how.* But I actual did it. In ten minutes I returned,
leading dear old cooperative Black Thunder, and wondering why I was going nuts. Soup was crazy. This I'd known for
years. I must also be a flicko, or why would he and I be such
close pals? Loony birds of a feather flick together.

Ox and Janice returned.

Using rope and harness, we hitched Black Thunder to the
front, then the four of us pushed from behind, and we
moved it. Right to the brink of Dugan's Hill. Luckily we

stopped. One more inch and nothing (not even Black Thunder) could have stopped our <u>Eat at Joe's</u> red-hearted valentine box . . . on two toboggans and fresh snow. Not down Dugan's Hill.

"Yikes," said Soup, as he unhitched Black Thunder, "here comes trouble."

He pointed.

We all looked and saw Mr. Joe Spazzatura. "Hey," he was hollering. "Somebody stole my horse."

"Quick," said Soup, "we'll all hide inside the crate. Maybe Joe won't be able to find our secret door, and he'll take his horse, and go."

We hid inside.

But he found us. In charged Mr. Joe Spazzatura. In a scolding mood. Yet he didn't come alone. Someone else came in too, just to be with his owner and friend.

Black Thunder.

Even an extra-large refrigerator crate can sometimes become instantly overcrowded, I then observed. Because there we all were, inside, Soup and Ox and Janice and Joe and Black Thunder and me. Plus a thousand valentines.

Maybe it was gravity.

Or perhaps a sudden gust of north wind.

I felt us move. Only an inch, yet it was certain a movement. The crate, with all of us inside, slowly began to slide. The others didn't seem to notice. But I did. They were all too busy shouting accusations or whining apologies.

Thunder was doing neither. He was too absorbed in nibbling at the large pile of valentines.

Down the hill we started.

Everyone, including Black Thunder, leaped for the door. Our secret door. But it opened *in*, not out. So, in the ensuing crushing pileup, there was no escape.

Faster we sped . . . down . . . down the very longest and steepest grade in the entire county.

Dugan's Hill.

Fourteen

"Trapped," said Soup.

"What'll we do?" I asked him.

"If we do anything, it's gotta be *now*. Rob, let's put Plan A into action. It had better work. We don't have a Plan B."

I leaped to the front porthole, poked my head out, only to feel a blast of February air against my face. Soup, meanwhile, had grabbed the canoe paddle.

"Where are we?" he yelped.

"In bad trouble," I answered over my shoulder.

"Are we going straight down?" We were, until our favorite white horse decided to shift his weight. "Tell me," Soup was shouting. "Rob, we're not heading for any of the telephone poles, are we?"

"No."

"What are we headed for?"

Squinting, I tried to see clearly. But the cold Vermont air was watering my eyes. Plus the fact that the light, feathery snow was spraying up from the two curly prows of our red-and-white candy-cane toboggans.

Something loomed ahead.

A structure.

Perhaps, I was now thinking, our Plan A wouldn't work. Plan B, therefore, would be for Soup and me to leave town. Forever. And we would probable leave in an ambulance.

As our speed increased, everybody seemed to be hollering louder, in total panic. Luckily for Soup and me, we had earlier decided to use port-or-starboard hand signals. Even though both my hands were in mittens.

Blinking through the snow, I sudden saw what lay ahead of us, directly in our path.

Joe's Diner & Diesel Fuel Stop.

"Turn," I screamed to Soup.

"Which way?"

Looking ahead, I waved a frantic mitten, neither knowing nor caring whether it was a starboard or a port, hoping that Soup and his idiotic canoe paddle could somehow divert our suicidal course. To be factual, it wasn't Soup's paddle. It belonged to Mr. Roodermyer.

"Are we turning?" Soup bellowed.

"Yes, but the wrong way."

Ahead of us, Joe's Diner became closer and bigger, growing and approaching at an increasing speed. With luck, we'd miss the railroad dining car that was Mr. Joe Spazzatura's eatery.

We missed it. Sort of. Yet I heard a *hiss*, as though a snake was in the crate with us.

How, I will never know, but Soup's rudder managed to change our direction just enough so that we only gave Joe's Diner a glancing blow on its uphill side. I think we only dislodged Joe's sign.

Onward we slid.

Faster. Faster. Faster.

A foreign object suddenly sailed into the open roof of our crate. Joe's sign. Or rather, part of it. All it said was Eat at.

As snow was blowing and wind was whipping, I couldn't see a blessed thing. Ahead of us, I knew, was the village of Learning, where a Valentine's Day outdoor celebration was probable now in full swing. A pity we had most of the valentine cards.

Behind me, Ox and Janice were moaning and groaning in absolute terror (or trying to sing a hymn), and Joe Spazzatura was looking at his sign and saying what I imagined were unflattering remarks about Soup and me. Now, for certain, I'd be hanged as a horse thief. Or a sign thief. If I lived.

Forward we flew.

Inside the zooming crate, panic reigned supreme.

Nobody talked. They all shouted, cried, wept, prayed, or giggled hysterically, and sang a bar or two of "Nearer, My

God, to Thee." Black Thunder, now prancing and bucking, was having a joyous time kicking Janice, which I enjoyed watching.

Janice kicked back.

Down we slid, gaining speed.

We had reached, I knew, the very steepest section of Dugan's Hill, a location local citizens referred to as Dead Man's Ledge.

Here, the road narrowed to cross over a small and rickety one-way bridge. Motorcycles (driven only by the young or the recklessly rash) sometimes, but only in summer, attempted to climb *up* Dugan's Hill. But not even the most foolhardy of dimwits ever attempted going *down.*

And here we were, helplessly racing to our doom, to some unknown obstacle below, waiting to abruptly halt and terminally shatter what was merely intended to be Miss Boland's big box to hold valentines. I remembered a skier, named Dugan; and in my stomach, my dear sweet mother's now half-digested pancakes and buttermilk were threatening a revolting reversal.

"Where are we?" Soup called.

"You don't want to know," I said.

Ahead I could see people, cars, trucks, children, and dogs, all occupying the modest little street where Soup had insisted that our moronic valentine crate would glide harmless to a stop.

Our speed increased.

With my head through the square porthole, it seemed we were heading straight down, as though sliding down the inside wall of an elevator shaft.

Soup hollered, "Where are we going, Rob?"

"I can't tell for sure," I screamed, "but wherever it is, we're getting there in about five seconds."

During each second, we doubled our rate of speed. Roadside trees now flew by like bullets. The seconds ticked off, as seconds do, one by one by one, as I prayed for a quick and painless death.

Five . . . four . . . three . . . two . . . one.

We hit the lip of a snowdrift.

I never dreamed, not even during the wildest fantasies of my imagination, that old Black Thunder could fly. Yet there he was, somewhere in midair, hoofs flailing. Mr. Joe Spazzatura was on Black Thunder's back, waving his apron, and yodeling in Italian.

I didn't see Soup.

Janice Riker and Oxide Heartburn were flipping over and over, but still holding hands. As I flew through the crispy Vermont ozone, head over heels, I thought I spotted Joe leaving his horse, both arms waving for balance, now riding his sign as if it were a surfboard.

I heard gasps from the crowd.

Below me, upturned faces stared wide-eyed, their jaws drooping and their mouths agape in alarm.

I saw Mrs. Edna Culpepper point away up at Joe on his sign. "Goodness," she said, "I'd hate to be up there on *that thing*."

Her husband, Malbert, snorted in his usual arid monotone. "Well," he said. "I'd hate to be up there without it."

One by one, we landed. I landed first.

Soup landed on me. That wasn't much fun at all. But to

balance out the day's disaster, there was one pleasing sight. Joe and Oxide and Black Thunder all crashed on Janice. But hardly all at once. Properly spaced. No sooner had she picked herself up from one encounter, another would descend upon her. Janice Riker, during her career, had given a lot of us kids a lot of licks. So she had it coming.

Soup found his stolen rudder, the canoe paddle.

Smiling, he handed it to its owner. "Here you are, Mr. Roodermyer," said Soup. "I'd like to give you back your paddle."

Mr. Roodermyer reclaimed it. "And now," he told Soup, "I'm going to give your back my paddle." Grabbing Soup, he gave his backside one smarting *whack*!

Our refrigerator crate (or, to be more accurate, Joe's) lay in a splintery demolished heap. The only part of it still intact was Soup's beautiful and ingenious combination of a triangle and a B. The red heart seemed to have miraculously survived.

But everything had not yet come to earth.

Above our heads, a thousand white valentines floated in the breeze, dropping slowly as would falling leaves, a festive snowstorm of seasonal wishes. As each valentine fell, an eager hand stretched upward to meet it and greet it, then forward it to its proper recipient.

There were valentines for everyone.

Janice received an extra-large one from Oxide Heartburn and began, I could see, to recover. Soup was flanked by both Quickie and Trickie, the twins, and appeared to be pulled in two directions. I imagined it could be a real kick to have both arms yanked from their sockets at the same time.

Longingly, I searched for Norma Jean Bissell.

Again I heard another *hiss*. I'd heard it yesterday, at the railroad station when the train had released its air brakes and was leaving. The *hissing* came again. Louder. This was impossible. It was February, and there were no snakes around in winter. Also, it was the wrong day for a noon train to arrive, so there were no railroad cars in town.

But hold on. There wasn't a train in Learning, yet there was *one railroad car.*

That's when I was final rewarded by the most eye-catching, attention-getting scene of my brief but entire lifetime experience. Seeing it, I could now look at nothing else. What I saw was occurring over halfway up Dugan's Hill. Bug-eyed, I watched a certain well-known railroad car move, on its track.

Joe's Diner rolled toward us.

Fifteen

Soup pointed.

"Rob, look what's coming."

"I'm looking."

So was everyone in town. The final *hiss*, made by the ancient railroad dining car, caught everyone's attention. There was no way to stop a railroad car, not when the air brake released its hold.

"Watch out," people were screaming. "Here it comes."

Children cried, women wept, and lumberjacks fainted in a swoon. We all knew the inevitable. Down it rolled, down the steepest part of Dugan's Hill, along its track. The railroad track ended right here, close to where we all now stood, at the wall of an old deserted building.

Peterson's Paint Factory.

Even before Soup and I were born (or so our town historian recorded) old Jonibiah Peterson died, leaving no heirs. When he died, his paint factory died with him. Years passed, and our village elders constantly discussed a possibility of letting our local eyesore, Peterson's Paint Factory, fall victim to a wrecking ball.

Everyone talked.

No one acted.

And now, as I stood spellbound and speechless, Joe's Diner was gaining speed. Steel wheels screamed along the rusty, unused iron rails . . . a witch's cry.

"I can't look," said Soup.

Yet he did. I did.

So did every single eye in Learning.

Down it came. Down. Down . . . until the ending final happened, as Joe's met Peterson's.

KEE-RASHBOOMBANGSMASHANDBAM-TINKLETINKLE.

As earlier the sky above our town had been filled with floating and falling valentines, it now filled with loose-lid paint cans. All sizes. Apparently, on the last day of its operation, the factory had been manufacturing paint. (At Peterson's, they made all colors.) But now, only the last working day's color could be seen!

Red.

Upon the white snows of Vermont sprayed blotches, puddles, specks, streaks, blots, and blobs of bright red paint.

"At last," I heard Miss Boland's voice remarking, in her usual cheery spirit, "our town is color-coordinated for Valentine's Day."

Paint and paintbrushes seemed to be everywhere.

Much of the red paint, however, now frosted the roof and sides of Joe's Diner. The factory didn't survive the crash, but the diner seemed to be still in order . . . in its new downtown location.

"Let's have a bonfire," someone said.

In no time, people scooped up the busted boards of Joe's old refrigerator crate, and a toasty fire blazed away. A welcome treat on a cold day.

Black Thunder seemed to be enjoying it, too, as the old white horse (now partly red) calmly grazed on an unclaimed valentine . . . until it was rescued by Miss Kelly.

She opened it, because her name was on it.

"Oh," she said, "it's from *Joe!*"

Miss Boland also got a valentine from Joe, and was as pleased as a parsnip. I happened to find *my* valentine, and presented it to my one and only heart of hearts, Norma Jean Bissell. My reward was another round at a favorite new game.

Soup was right.

It was better than baseball.

Well, it was doggone near almost as good.

"Say," said Miss Kelly, "let's all grab a paintbrush, and use some of the leftover red paint, and finish the job on Joe's Diner."

"Super idea," said Miss Boland, who then didn't actual do

any of the painting herself, but served in a supervisory capacity.

We all painted.

The diner sign now only said <u>Joe's</u>. Nobody could find the <u>Eat at</u> part. However, in no time at all, the downtown diner began to look totally red and spiffy, and just about everyone promised to become one of Joe's future customers.

But I couldn't find Joe.

No one could.

We looked everywhere, and kept calling his name, but there was no clue to Joe's whereabouts. Then he appeared, coming out of the door of his diner, quite alive, and petting his kitten.

"She is safe," he said. "But I still need a name for her. Who's got a name for my new kitten?"

"Valentina," I said.

Joe smiled at me. "You win a prize, Rob," he said, "and here it is. A photograph of a very well-known horse."

He handed me the picture.

It was Black Thunder.

"And," Joe said, "now for the prize for the most original valentine. The prize, ladies and gentlemen, is dinner for two at the new Joe's Diner, located in downtown Learning . . . the prize goes to . . ."

The crowd held its collective breath.

". . . to Luther Vinson."

Soup smirked. "Ah," he said, "I won," as he collected the two-free-dinners certificate from Mr. Joe Spazzatura.

"Not so fast," said Ox. "We now gonna have a good-time, old-fashioned, down-home stomping and picking *Texas-style* taffy pull." He reached out a giant paw to grab Soup Vinson. "And son," he firmly stated with a wide western smile, "you're fixing to be the *taffy*."

All of a sudden, Quickie and Trickie appeared, each twin taking a firm purchase on Soup's hair.

"Pull," said Ox.

They pulled.

Soup was yelping. It did him little good.

For several long seconds, I didn't think that Luther Wesley Vinson would remain assembled in one piece. Quickie yanked one way, Trickie the other. Sooner or later, something had to snap; because, between the twins, Soup was stretching like a sleepy cat.

"Hold it," said Mr. Joe Spazzatura. "I make a big mistake. The prize I meant to award was" . . . (he smiled) . . . "dinner for *three*."

Everyone applauded. Quickie and Trickie seemed to be satisfied, and the whole town returned to romance.

Janice kissed Ox.

Quickie and Trickie hugged Soup.

Norma Jean Bissell and I, now into innings three, four, and five (even though I wasn't a lefty), resumed our new-improved game of Advanced Smooch.

Texas style!

This meant Norma Jean's rules.

And, as I could see from a corner of my eye, Miss Boland and Miss Kelly and Mr. Joe Spazzatura were dancing. Yes, actual *dancing* in the snow. Joe was still holding tight to his precious new kitten.

He seemed to be so happy that he was crying.

Joe and his diner had, in a way, come home. As I looked at him in his raggy clothes and scruffy wet shoes with knotted laces, I realized that our little town of Learning had been given the most wonderful human valentine of all.

There he stood.

Our jewel.

Mr. Joe Spazzatura, with a kitten and a pair of old friends, plus a new location where a lot of steady patrons would <u>Eat at Joe's</u> . . . as long as he lived.

Joe also had one thing more, a valentine that no one could actual see, yet everyone would always love.

The best and biggest heart.